SPOOK SUMMER

Mary Hooper

Illustrations by Susan Hellard

Galaxy

CHIVERS PRESS
BATH

First published 2001
by
Walker Books Ltd
This Large Print edition published by
Chivers Press
by arrangement with
Walker Books Ltd
2002

ISBN 0 7540 7811 6

British Library Cataloguing in Publication Data

Hooper, Mary,
Spook Summer.—Large print ed.
1. Children's stories 2. Large type books
I. Title
823. 9'14[J]

ISBN 0-7540-7811-6

Printed and bound in Great Britain by
BOOKCRAFT, Midsomer Norton, Somerset

CONTENTS

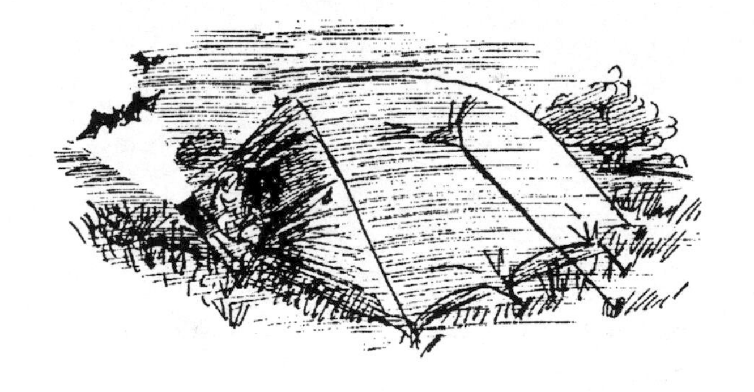

CHAPTER ONE

I sat on my bulging rucksack and bounced around a bit, just to squash everything down.

Mum gave a scream. 'I've just ironed all that lot! By the time you unpack, those clothes will look no good for anything!'

I rolled my eyes. 'I'm going camping, Mum! No one will have things that are ironed—it would be too embarrassing. Besides, I won't be unpacking. We haven't got wardrobes and chests of drawers in the tents, you know. Everything will be staying in my rucksack.'

Mum put on a pained expression. 'I can just see your clothes after a week: muddy things in with clean stuff, smelly trainers in with your pyjamas, wet swimsuit rolling around with next day's knickers . . .'

'I expect so,' I said cheerfully.

Our class at school—the top juniors—were going camping in a field for a week. The oldest class went every year, boys at the beginning of June and girls at the end, and when you came back you had to write up the week for your summer project, with illustrations and photographs and, if you were that way inclined, pressed flowers and stuff.

'Now, I've bought you a nice new notebook,' Mum said, producing it. 'It's got little pockets stuck on the pages so you can tuck in feathers and leaves and things.'

I looked at it in disgust. 'It's got daisies on it,' I said. 'It's got MY NATURE DIARY in green sparkly letters.'

'Yes,' Mum said. 'What's wrong with that?'

'I want a black book,' I said. 'A black book with mysterious signs and symbols and on the front'—I gave a harsh laugh—'DEADLY AND SPOOKY ENCOUNTERS. OPEN ON PENALTY OF DEATH.'

'Don't be silly,' Mum said. She tutted at me. 'I thought you might have got over all that spooky nonsense by now. You didn't find any spooks on our narrowboat trip—you didn't even get one in the castle you went to with Hannah.'

I looked at her witheringly.

'I bet Hannah's going to do this camping project properly. I bet she's looking forward to some lovely bird-spotting.'

I didn't bother to reply, just repeated the wither. Hannah was my best friend and she was mad on birds. Twitchers, they call people who bird-spot, and yes, Hannah was going to be super-twitching while we were away. She was taking six bird books with her, and her entire summer project was going to be about them. It always was. She lived and breathed little fluttery things.

I picked up my camera to put into my small day rucksack along with my washing stuff. I'd been given the camera for Christmas and it had a special filter so I could take pictures at night without a flash. Over the years I'd found that flash bulbs tended to put off ghosts and spirits—I'd never managed to photograph one yet—but with my new camera I had high hopes of getting something mysterious on film. A long-dead monk preferably, but I was open to anything the slightest bit spooky.

'You're not going to find any ghosts to hunt down there, anyway,' Mum said. 'You'll be miles from anywhere with cows for neighbours.'

'That's where you're wrong!' I crowed. 'Just up the hill there's the ruins of an abbey!'

'Oh, yes?'

'And I spoke to a girl who went last year and she said that strange noises come from the abbey, and lights are seen after midnight.' I shivered dramatically. 'The ghosts of long-dead monks walk in the moonlight!'

Mum smirked. 'That's all a bit old hat now,' she said. 'There are much trendier things than long-dead monks. I'm surprised you haven't got into them.'

I frowned. 'What d'you mean? What things?'

'You're going to Wiltshire, aren't you?'

I nodded.

'Well, that's where lots of crop

circles appear.'

'What's crop circles?' I asked suspiciously.

'Don't you know? They're big circles and signs left in the cornfields. Some people say they're made by aliens, some say they're made by freak winds.'

'I say aliens!' I said swiftly.

'And Wiltshire is also the place where aliens are supposed to land in their flying saucers—there are several hills where people swear they've seen them.'

'Really?' I asked, quite intrigued. I mean, I still liked spooks best—spooks were a lot more interesting, much *spookier* than aliens, but I never minded having more than one mysterious thing on the go at the same time. In this book I'd just read, the heroine had had about twelve adventures, one after the other—*everything* happened to her—so all I could say was if I didn't have at least four adventures when I was away then it was a pretty bad show.

'And there's that great big cat that has been seen on the moors. The Beast of Bodmin, they call it.'

'What sort of great big cat?'

'A great black panther,' Mum said. 'But I think that's away in Cornwall. Further south-west.'

'Is it a ghost?' I asked, interested. 'A ghost animal returning to avenge people?'

Mum shrugged. 'I don't really know. It could be a real animal that's escaped from a zoo, or it could be supernatural.' She flung up her arms. 'Whoo-ooo!'

'Don't be silly,' I said.

'You'd better keep your tent done up at night, just in case.'

'If it was a supernatural being,' I said, 'a bit of canvas would hardly stop it. Besides, Beezie will protect us.'

'Is that Miss Beasley? Is she the student teacher in charge of your tent?'

I nodded. 'Beastly Beezie: half beast, half woman.'

'Amy!'

'She's in with me and Hannah and Sasha and Sammy,' I said, pulling a face of disgust.

'What are Sasha and Sammy like?'

Mum asked. She was stripping the sheets off my bed by this time—stripping it and I hadn't even left the house! Talk about wanting to get rid of me.

'Drips,' I said.

Mum sighed. 'I'm sure they're very nice girls. Sensible girls.'

'Drips,' I muttered again under my breath.

Mum looked thoughtful. 'And the other thing people sometimes find in the country—in ploughed-up fields and so on—is treasure. They have metal detectors and they go round and when the detector gives a little whistle—'

'Treasure!' I interrupted. 'What sort of treasure? Big wooden chests containing pearls and diamonds and gold bars?'

'I don't think so,' Mum said. 'It's usually just old coins and sometimes pieces of rare pottery, stuff like that.' She looked at her watch. 'What time's the minibus coming?'

'Ten o'clock.'

Mum nodded. 'And are you sure you've got everything?'

'Mmm,' I said thoughtfully. I'd *thought* I had, but after listening to Mum I intended to take a few extra things with me. She went downstairs and I had a rummage round my bedroom, then stashed a few bits in the top zipped compartment of my big rucksack. At least I'd make sure that everyone in my tent had an interesting week . . .

CHAPTER TWO

We'd arrived in two minibuses. We were somewhere in Wiltshire, in the middle of a field. There were eighteen girls, five teachers, an assortment of tents, something called a Portaloo—which was actually loos and washbasins—and a covered wooden trailer with all the food in it. We were surrounded by hills, a river and, across a field and up a hill, the deliciously crumbly and spooky-looking ruins of the abbey.

Inside our tent there were five campbeds, a pile of rucksacks and a jumble of clothes. The air was pale green, warm and muggy. I was busy telling Sammy and Sasha—and Hannah, when she occasionally looked up from her bird books—about the interesting, dangerous and spooky things nearby.

'On top of that hill'—I pointed vaguely out of the tent—'is where the flying saucers land. So if you go up there you must be careful that you don't get taken away.'

Sasha and Sammy looked at me nervously.

I made a low humming sound under my breath without moving my lips. 'I think that's a flying saucer right now . . .' I said, but of course to speak I had to stop doing the humming noise.

I started it again and Sasha popped her head out of the tent and then popped it back in again. 'Funny. It seems louder inside the tent,' she said.

I stopped humming again. 'That's because of the echo effect.'

'And it seems to stop every time you speak,' Sammy said.

'That's . . . that's because I'm being used as a medium,' I said, not at all sure what that actually meant.

'I don't think I'll go out at all,' Sammy said. 'What with the headless monks gliding along in the moonlight . . .'

'And the black panthers leaping out of the hedges,' Sasha continued.

'Not to mention the mysterious crop circles,' Hannah put in.

'You just stick close to me and you'll be all right,' I said. 'I have ways of dealing with alien life-forces.' I pretended to look over my shoulder fearfully. 'Between you and me, though, it's the mysterious black panther that gives me the creeps. Big as a house, it's supposed to be.'

Beezie put her head in the door flap of our tent and we all jumped.

'I hope you're not scaring everyone with your silly stories, Amy,' she said.

I smiled tightly.

'Don't take any notice of Amy,' she said to everyone else. 'There's absolutely nothing to be scared of here. The worst thing that can happen is that you get stung by a nettle.'

'Or pounced on by the Beast of Bodmin or caught up in a vortex of a crop circle,' I said softly. I wasn't quite sure what this last thing was either, but it sounded good.

Beezie lumbered into the tent and crashed down onto her campbed. She was as big as a wardrobe, with long frizzy hair that stuck out everywhere.

'The only thing any of you have to

worry about is getting on the wrong side of the local landowner, Mr Dean,' Beezie said. 'Apparently he's a bit of an ogre.'

'Really?' I said. 'What, a real ogre? Like a big huge giant?'

Beezie ignored me. 'Mr Dean owns most of the land round here, apart from the field we're in. We've got to be very careful not to trespass—if we're going through fields or down to the river we must skirt round the edges *very carefully*.'

I yawned. I'd heard all this before, earlier, from Mrs Emmet, who was the teacher in charge of the whole visit. Apparently if a blade of Mr Dean's grass was flattened he'd stop us from coming here ever again, if a sweet-wrapper was dropped on his land he'd sue the school to within an inch of its life, and if anyone touched a tree he'd kill them. Practically, anyway.

'I've never met him, this information has just been passed down over the last five years we've been coming here,' Mrs Emmet had said. 'But we've had very strong letters sent to the school whenever we've done something even slightly out of turn. If we want to continue our country visits, we must all treat his land with great care.'

'Have you been listening, Amy?' Beezie said when she'd finished the recitation of what we could and couldn't do.

I nodded. I was wondering whether I could get out at night—in the middle of the night—without Beezie knowing. And I was wondering whether to head for the big hill I'd noticed with the flattish top where aliens were going to land, or stick to hunting down my old favourites: ghosts and ghouls.

* * *

Dusk was falling and I'd volunteered me and Hannah to collect wood to start the camp-fire, so we were going around the edges of the far side of the big field we were camped in, looking in the ditch for likely pieces of twiggle. Hannah wasn't being much help at all, trailing behind me with her nose in a bird book and every so often saying,

'There's a goldfinch,' or, 'Just look at that warbler.'

Across the lane, over the hedge and up the hill loomed the abbey—or what was left of it. Just the front and back bits were standing: two great curved stone arches where the stained glass windows had once been. Behind the abbey, the full moon shone with a pale and sinister light.

'Look!' I breathed. 'Are those black ravens flying in and out cawing to each other—or are they the souls of the long-dead monks?'

Hannah glanced up. 'I'm impressed!' she said. '*Ravens.* You got them right.'

'But hark!' I said. 'What's that unearthly cry that pierces the night?'

Hannah harked. 'That's Mrs Emmet starting the camp-fire singsong,' she said. 'We'd better get back.'

I grabbed her arm. 'Will you dare to come back here with me in the darkest, shiveriest hour?'

'And miss the sausage and bean bake?' she said. 'No fear.'

I sighed. 'Sometimes I wonder why you're my best friend.'

*   *   *

By eleven o'clock we'd finished eating and singing jolly songs and were getting ready for bed. While the others were still cleaning their teeth in the Portaloos, though, I was back in the tent getting the first interesting diversion out of the secret pocket of my rucksack. This consisted of (a) my cardboard cut-out cat—a 'perfect pet' that Mum had given me for Christmas—and (b) my super-powerful torch. Carefully, I stood the cardboard cat near to the canvas wall of the tent, then put the torch under my campbed and directed its beam straight onto the cat.

I went outside to look. Fantastic! It looked *huge*—like the Beast of Bodmin, only bigger.

I went over to the Portaloo and walked back with Hannah, Sammy and Sasha. Our tent was the last one in the line of six, next to the end hedge, so it wasn't until you'd passed the other tents that you could see the big cat in its full glory.

I pointed and clutched Hannah's arm. 'Oh, my God! Look at that dreadful huge beast in our tent!'

Sasha and Sammy let out a joint scream. Hannah, more used to my little ways, didn't.

I struck a terrified pose, arms raised in horror. 'It must be the Beast of Bodmin!' I shrieked.

Sasha and Sammy clutched each other.

'Get Beezie!' Sasha cried.

'Call the police!' Sammy screamed.

Hannah looked at me. 'Is it the Beast of Bodmin?' she asked.

'Possibly,' I said. 'Or it could be the Wildcat of Wiltshire.'

Beezie bore down on us in plaid woolly dressing-gown and sheepskin slippers, having already changed for bed in the Portaloo. 'What's all this noise?' she said. 'And why is it always my girls? All the others are quiet and peaceful.'

Sasha pointed. 'Horrible furry beast, Miss!' she quavered.

'Sasha,' I whispered, 'is that any way

to talk about Miss Beasley?'

No one heard me. 'What are you talking about?' Beezie asked, looking all around her. 'What furry beast?'

By then I was halfway to the tent, and by the time Sammy said, 'It's over there. In our tent, Miss!' I'd reached it, snatched up my torch and pushed the cardboard cat flat under my sleeping-bag.

I went back to the tent flap and looked out. 'It's OK!' I called to them. 'I think I've scared it off.'

'What on earth was it?' Beezie said as she came nearer with Sammy and Sasha cowering behind her.

'Just a black panther,' I said carelessly. 'A great girl-eating black panther. The Wildcat of Wiltshire, I think they call it.'

Sammy clutched at Beezie. 'I'm not sleeping in there, Miss!'

Beezie marched into the tent followed by Hannah, who was giving me one of her looks.

'I hope this isn't anything to do with you, Amy,' Beezie said severely. 'I trust that you heeded what I said to you earlier and . . .' Her sharp beastly eyes suddenly spotted something and she bent over my campbed. 'Aha,' she said. 'There's a cardboard tail sticking out from under your sleeping-bag. Perhaps you can explain yourself . . .'

CHAPTER THREE

'I don't care,' I said to Hannah. 'I'd rather stay here peeling potatoes. Who wants to go on a nature trail, anyway?'

'Going out in big numbers is never a good thing,' Hannah muttered. 'Every bird within two miles will just be scared off.'

It was the following morning and, as punishment for frightening Sasha and Sammy to death, I'd been chosen to help Miss Powling, one of the other teachers, peel the day's potatoes. These would be cooked later, with meat and onions and stuff, in a great big stewpot over a fire—and pretty revolting it sounded too.

The potatoes and all the other food were in the trailer which had been attached to Mrs Emmet's car, and Miss Powling sent me off to collect them. We'd had to bring all the food we'd need for the week with us, because there were no shops nearby. No anything nearby, really.

I collected the potatoes and looked around. We were using up about half of a big field, and surrounding us on each side were high hedges tangled with bushes and briars and wild flowers. There were two five-bar gates in the field: one leading out onto the lane we'd come along in our minibus and the other onto a muddy path which led down to the river. We weren't allowed to go near the river without a teacher, of course, in case we drowned ourselves accidentally.

I yawned. I hadn't slept that well, because I'd kept waking up and thinking I could hear animals scratching at the tent in the night. They'd sounded like panthers, I thought—but I couldn't tell Beezie that, could I? Instead, I'd tried to keep my mind off it by planning what to say to aliens if I actually met them. I mean, I wanted to speak to them, but I didn't want to have to go back to their planet with them or anything.

The others went off on the nature trail with Sammy and Sasha smirking at me in a prissy, goody-goody way and

Beezie saying something about hoping I'd learned my lesson.

Miss Powling and I made short work of the potatoes and then she said I could do my own thing as long as I stayed within earshot, because she wanted some time to herself to do what sounded like 'fungshway the tent'.

I looked at her blankly. 'Is that one of those fluffy dogs?'

'No,' she said. And she spelt out, 'FENG SHUI. It's the placement of objects to increase the flow of energies. For instance, at the moment my campbed is placed with the head towards the north and it needs to be changed. And my chair is facing the tent flap, which is a very negative position and means all my luck will flow out of the door.' She closed her eyes. 'I need to feel the positive forces and act accordingly.'

'I see,' I said politely. And Mum thinks *I'm* mad.

I went back to the tent and consulted the little map we'd been given of where everything was, which showed the places we could and couldn't go. The ruined abbey was OK, it wasn't on the ogre farmer's land or anything, so I set off towards it, going down the lane a bit, over a stile and then across a couple of fields.

I walked up a sloping field with corn nearly up to my waist. This, according to my map, belonged to Mr Dean the demon farmer, but as instructed in big letters I KEPT TO THE SIDE OF THE FIELDS BEING CAREFUL NOT TO TREAD ON ANY CROP until I reached the top. I then came to a small wooded and fenced area on a hill called Hangman's Hill, which was also owned by him, and then the abbey stood on the top of the next slope.

The hill beyond that was the one with a flattish top, which looked to me as if it might be suitable for alien landings. I made up my mind I'd investigate it as soon as possible.

Standing next to the abbey wall, I glanced down towards the field we were camped in. I could just about see the tops of the tents but I wasn't sure if I was out of earshot of Miss Powling or not—I suppose this depended how loudly she could shout. I'd got this far, though, so nothing (save for aliens) was going to keep me out of the ruins.

Disappointingly, this was all they were: *ruins*. Just crumbly piles of stonework, all overgrown with nettles and clumps of grass. I'd hoped there might have been a proper room left standing somewhere there, a room with grey stone walls, a big old table and perhaps a skeleton of a monk sitting at it, but there wasn't. In fact, apart from the two tall end walls of the church, there wasn't much to see at all.

But that didn't mean there weren't ghosts there at night, of course. Ghosts and ghouls. Ghosts didn't need proper rooms to waft round, they could do it quite nicely in the moonlight. Better, I should think.

I carried on investigating and, after looking very hard, found a tall, thin stone that, if you used every ounce of your imagination and squished your eyes up small, could have once been a monk. I took three photographs ('A mysterious monk turned into stone by an evil witch' I'd write underneath it in my project-book) and went back to our camp.

As I arrived, the others were just coming in from the nature ramble. Sasha proudly showed me her project-book which had a few drippy leaves and a piece of corn stuck to the pages, and Sammy had the same, with the addition of half a chicken's feather. Hannah had lots of birds listed with some pen-and-ink sketches underneath: great spotted woodpeckers and stuff like that—quite good, actually. Mine would be better, of course.

CHAPTER FOUR

After lunch, which was bread and cheese, we were allowed to go off exploring. We could either go down to the river with a couple of teachers, or go along the lane and see what we could find in the hedgerows. When we heard the bell that Mrs Emmet was going to ring for tea we had to come back. Most of the others chose to go down to the river, but I persuaded Hannah that she ought to climb up the hill beyond the abbey with me. I wanted to look for evidence (scorched grass? big, round flat mark?) of landings.

'You'll see all sorts of birds on the way,' I said persuasively. 'Things you've never seen before. Exotic birds. Penguins and stuff.'

She looked at me hard. 'Penguins?'

'Well, maybe not penguins,' I said. 'Everything except them.'

We set off by the same route I'd taken that morning. I walked towards the abbey so I could show Hannah the monk turned into stone on the way. I also wanted to try out some haunted abbey tales on her: tales of ghouls and spectres and spirits. Those she thought were the spookiest I was going to tell after lights out and before Beezie came to bed, and terrify Sasha and Sammy.

We didn't get as far as that, though. Going past the wooded copse, Hannah suddenly gave a cry.

I brandished my camera. 'Is it an alien?'

'No! I've just seen a pied flycatcher. Really, I have!'

'Is that good or bad?' I asked.

'It's good. It's *excellent*,' she said. 'They're summer visitors and quite rare in this part of the country.'

'There you are, then,' I said. 'Aren't you glad you came with me?'

'I want to see it again!' She stood by the wire fence, peering into the wood. 'I want to know whether it's a male or female.'

I looked at her in amazement. 'What for? Who cares?'

'I do,' she said. 'I want to know if it's

male or female and if it's nesting in there.'

I looked longingly towards the next hill. 'Do you *have* to?' I asked plaintively. 'I want to get up to the alien landing-place.'

'It's terribly important to me . . .'

'Well, apart from anything else, you're not allowed,' I said. 'This little wood belongs to the demon farmer. It's forbidden land.'

She gave a wail—and then we saw a figure coming towards us from the other side of the copse. I wish I could say it was someone interesting like a monk, or even the demon farmer, but it wasn't. It was just a woman wearing a green padded jacket, with a pair of binoculars and a camera round her neck.

Hannah immediately recognized her as a fellow twitcher, don't ask me how.

'I just saw a pied flycatcher go into those trees!' Hannah said to her.

'No! That's amazing.'

'I was just telling my friend. Have you ever seen one here before?'

The woman shook her head.

'Never—and I'm around all the time. Are you sure about the colouring?'

Hannah nodded. 'Brown and white, clear white wing bar.'

'That's right! About thirteen centimetres long. Fantastic!'

While they droned on I looked towards the alien landing hill. If we hung about much longer, old Emmet would be ringing her bell and we'd have to go back.

'Why don't you go into the copse and check,' the woman said to Hannah. 'You can go under this wire.'

'You mustn't, Hannah!' I said quickly, thinking about reaching the alien landing-spot. 'We're not allowed. The land's owned by Mr Dean, the demon farmer, who kills people who go onto it.'

'Oh, surely not,' the woman said.

'He absolutely does,' I said. 'We've been told all about him—he's a wicked tyrant who holds the village people in terror of their lives.'

The woman looked at me strangely.

I grabbed Hannah's arm. 'Come on, let's get on,' I said.

She sighed. 'I'll probably never ever see another pied flycatcher as long as I live.'

'Wait a sec,' the woman said. 'Mr Dean's away at the moment.'

I looked at her suspiciously. 'Are you sure?'

The woman nodded. 'I live in the village. We locals know everything that goes on round here.'

'That's all right, then,' Hannah said, practically through the fence already.

'I'll tell you what,' the woman said, 'you go through and look for the pied flycatcher, and your friend and I will keep watch.' She smiled at me. 'I'm Julia, by the way. What are your names?'

We told her and she said it would be perfectly OK for Hannah to go through, that no one would know, and while Hannah was in there would I mind giving her a hand—she wanted to see how many fieldmice were in the cornfield we'd just been through.

Hannah disappeared into the copse and I looked at the woman—Julia—puzzled.

‘Fieldmice? What for?’

‘Oh, er—it’s to do with the owl population,’ she said. ‘It’s declining and we think it might be something to do with the numbers of mice—they’re the staple diet of owls, you know. It won’t take a moment. I just want to check over the field.’

She set off and I followed her, a bit bemused.

‘Are we allowed to go in this field?’ I said as we approached it. ‘Doesn’t it belong to the demon farmer?’

‘Oh, we’re not hurting it,’ Julia said. ‘And as I said, he’s away so he won’t know anyway.’ She advanced into the field, taking a length of rope out of her pocket. ‘Stay on the path by the hedge until I tell you to move, will you?’

I did as I was told, my mind still on the abbey. I was thinking that I might ask Julia if she’d ever heard anything spooky about it, any local myths and legends, when she called me over. She asked me to stand still, holding the rope, while she slowly walked in a circle around me, treading down the corn.

I looked over my shoulder fearfully. 'Are you supposed to do that?'

'Oh, no harm done,' she said. 'It can still be harvested. I'm just counting nests.'

She finished there, then we walked further down the field and she walked in another circle round me, then did the same thing two more times. It all looked mad to me, and not much like she was counting mouse nests or anything, but then twitchers are a bit strange. I've always known that, because of being friends with Hannah for ages.

When we got right to the bottom of the field she coiled up the rope and put it away. 'Thanks very much, Amy,' she said. 'That was very helpful.'

'That's all right,' I said. Barking, I thought. Just like Hannah.

We went up the sloping field again towards Hannah, who was now standing on our side of the fence, smiling all over her face.

'I've seen two!' she said. 'A breeding pair!'

'How marvellous,' said Julia. She

smiled at me. 'And we've had a successful time, too, haven't we, Amy?'

'If you say so,' I said.

Faintly, down in the valley where the tents were, we heard the sound of ringing.

'Oh, no!' I groaned. 'That's Mrs Emmet with the handbell!'

'We'd better go back,' Hannah said.

'But we haven't done the alien landing-strip yet! I haven't shown you the monk turned to stone.'

'He'll still be there tomorrow,' Hannah said, looking as happy as if she'd seen a penguin and an albatross having a tea party. 'And maybe I'll see the pied flycatchers again, too.'

'Oh, that *would* be thrilling,' I said.

When we got back I wrote in my nature diary: *Helped local woman with important project to do with owls and fieldmice, measuring the number of mouse nests in a cornfield.*

It wasn't alien landings, but at least that was a bit more interesting than finding a couple of leaves and half a feather.

*   *   *

That night, when Beezie was in Mrs Emmet's tent with the other teachers—having what they called 'their time off'—and we were tucked into our sleeping-bags, I had a delve into my rucksack and started telling Hannah and Sasha and Sammy a tale about a witch that I just happened to know lived in the nearby village.

'This witch lived in a hollowed-out oak tree and only came out when the moon was full,' I said. Lowering my voice dramatically, I added, 'She was a very wicked witch who used to put spells on people. They'd go to bed OK but wake up covered in warts.'

Sammy shuddered. 'That would be like being covered in verrucas.'

'Did she ride on a broomstick?' Sasha asked.

'Sometimes,' I said. 'But mostly she rode on the back of a snowy owl.'

'Was it a *huge* snowy owl?' Hannah asked, interested. 'Or did the witch make herself small?'

I thought. 'She made herself small,' I

said. 'But she was quite small anyway, wasn't she, because she lived in a tree-trunk.'

'Yes. Course she was,' Hannah said.

'And when anyone in the village was nasty to her, she'd summon the owl and then she'd get on his back and together they'd swoop onto the person who'd been nasty, and she'd make magic signs over their cottage and drop something down their chimney, and in the morning they'd be covered with warts. And this went on until they caught her and burnt her at the stake.'

'When was this?' Hannah asked.

'I was just coming to that.' I struggled to remember the exact details of the book I'd just read. 'It was three hundred years ago . . . but they do say that once every year, on the anniversary of the day she died, you can hear her owl hooting mournfully.' I picked up the bird-call trick that I'd had in my Christmas stocking and blew into it.

Hoot . . . hoot . . . hoot . . .

'Hark! It's the anniversary this very night, and I do believe I can hear it now!'

Hoot . . . hoot . . . hoot . . .

There was complete silence from two beds, just the even breathing sound of two girls who were fast asleep, then Hannah asked, 'Did you say it was a snowy owl?'

'Yes.'

Hoot-hoot . . .

'Only that noise you're making is actually the call of a wood pigeon.'

I scowled at Hannah in the darkness. 'Oh, do be quiet,' I said.

CHAPTER FIVE

'Amy!' Mrs Emmet came up to me just as I was sitting outside our tent and thinking about getting the next item out of the secret compartment in my rucksack.

I shoved the rucksack behind my back. 'Yes, Mrs Emmet?'

'Two chaps have arrived here,' Mrs Emmet said, looking bemused and pointing somewhere behind her. 'They're from London newspapers and they want to know where Hangman's Hill is. Could you go with Miss Beasley and show them?'

I scrambled to my feet. 'Is it aliens?' I asked excitedly. 'Have they landed?'

'I don't think so, dear,' Mrs Emmet said. 'They haven't mentioned it, anyway.'

'They wouldn't!' I said. 'It would cause panic among the masses.'

'I'm perfectly sure it's not aliens,' Mrs Emmet said, rather sternly. I think she'd heard about the Wildcat of

Wiltshire. 'Just go and find Miss Beasley. The men are waiting at the gate.'

I found Beezie in the Portaloo. There were no showers, of course, and none of us lot were bothering to wash much anyway, but the teachers seemed to spend ages messing around with two inches of ice-cold water and a flannel. I gave Beezie the message from Mrs Emmet and then, with the rest of the girls looking at us curiously, we went over to the two men. They were called Ben and Jake and there wasn't much to choose between them. Both had cameras, hooded jackets and combat trousers.

'Is it aliens?' I said, as soon as I'd grabbed my camera and we were out of the gate. 'You can tell me. I won't tell anyone.'

Beezie gave an enormous laugh. 'Of course it's not aliens, silly!'

'Could be,' Ben said.

'It's crop circles, actually,' the other one said.

'And as no one in the world knows how they come about . . .'

'It could well be . . .'

'Aliens!'

I looked at Beezie triumphantly. Crop circles! I thought. It was a good job Mum had told me about them.

I pointed over a hedge into the first field. 'You go up here,' I said, going over the stile. 'I came up here to the abbey yesterday. I found a stone that had once been a monk.'

They didn't take much notice of this because they were chatting between themselves.

'If we get an exclusive,' the first one said.

'It's newsworthy stuff . . .'

'I'll split the fee with you . . .'

'Sell it on to the nationals . . .'

'Make a mint . . .'

I was so engrossed in listening to them and thinking of what I was going to write about crop circles in my project-book, that I missed the field we should have gone across and we got right up to Hangman's Hill without going through the cornfield.

Ben turned around slowly. 'Apparently the crop circles can be seen from the top of this hill.'

'Well, this is definitely Hangman's Hill,' I explained. 'And over there is the abbey with the monk turned into stone which I discovered personally myself yesterday.'

They didn't even *look* at the abbey.

'Hey—good circles!' Ben said suddenly.

'Cool!' said Jake.

I looked to where they were looking: the cornfield I'd been in the day before with Julia, the bird-watching woman. When we'd gone back to collect Hannah I hadn't bothered to look at it again, but now I did. I saw that right down its length were four perfectly round circles.

'Look at *those* for crop circles!' Ben said admiringly.

I gave a little strangled cry.

'For real!' Jake said, fixing a lens to his camera.

Beside me, Beezie gasped. 'How marvellous,' she said. 'Four perfect circles in the corn. However did they get there?'

Jake muttered under his breath,

'That's one of the mysteries . . .'

'Of the age,' Ben said, snapping away.

'But I . . .' I began. And then I shut up.

'Aren't you going to take photographs, Amy?' Beezie said. 'This is a golden opportunity for you.'

Half-heartedly I took one, and while I was putting my camera away Julia appeared, striding across a ploughed-up field in green wellies.

'Ah,' she said, 'I thought I might find you all here.'

I opened my mouth to say something. I wanted to say, 'Hey, they think those marks you made yesterday when you were counting fieldmice are crop circles . . .' but something about the way she looked at me, something about the way she winked, stopped me.

I introduced her to Beezie, and Beezie got all nervous, saying that she hoped we weren't trespassing and she wouldn't want to be reported to Mr Dean.

'No, that'll be quite all right,' Julia said. She turned to the men. 'Get a tip-off, did you?' she asked them.

'Sure did,' Ben said. 'Have you had crop circles here before?'

Julia shook her head.

'Well, I'm afraid you're going to get overrun with reporters now,' Ben said. 'There's not much regular news, and we do like a crop circle or two to keep us going in the silly season.'

'That's OK.' Julia was smiling. 'I'm going to charge every newspaper fifty pounds to come on my land, so I don't mind how many I get. The more the merrier!'

'But . . . er . . . isn't all this land owned by Mr Dean?' Beezie asked. 'And isn't he a bit fanatical about people straying where they shouldn't?'

'This land is owned by *Miss* Dean,' Julia said. 'That's me.'

We all stared at her. Ooh-er, I thought.

'Daniel Dean is my uncle, but he's retired and gone to live in Wales. I'm in charge now and I'll thank you reporter chaps for your fifty-pound entry fees, please.'

*   *   *

Back at the camp, Beezie went to report to Mrs Emmet and the others, while I went into my tent, got my nature diary and ripped out the page saying: *Helped local woman with important project to do with owls and fieldmice, measuring the number of mouse nests in a cornfield.* I tore it into small pieces and stuffed them in the bottom of my rucksack.

Sammy, Sasha and Hannah came rushing back.

'Mrs Emmet's just told us!' Hannah said.

'I can't believe it!' Sasha said. 'Crop circles. Just like you said, Amy!'

'Alien crop circles!' Sammy screeched.

'Er . . . yes,' I said.

'Did aliens land?' Sasha asked. 'Did they land and make them?'

'I expect so,' I said.

Hannah looked at me strangely. 'I thought you'd be full of it. I thought you'd have had a close encounter with them by now.'

I shrugged modestly. 'Not necessarily. I personally think these crop circles are a bit overrated. Aliens aren't nearly as exciting as ghosts.'

'Oh, I think they are!' Sammy said. 'ET's an alien! ET can do magic.'

'Ghosts can do . . . do *hauntings*!' I said, but she didn't look impressed.

*   *   *

Later, when we were getting ready for bed, Hannah got me on my own. 'There was something funny about those crop circles, wasn't there?'

'What? Why d'you think that?'

'Because you're not saying much about them.'

I shrugged. 'Maybe there is, and maybe there isn't.'

'Tell me,' she said, 'or I'll run through the names of every bird I've ever heard of, starting with avocet and ending with yellowhammer.'

'Well,' I said hastily, 'put it this way. If you discovered what you thought was a very rare and special bird, and then when you got close to it you found out that it was plastic, what would you do?'

She thought for a moment. 'Probably I'd keep quiet about it,' she said.

'Exactly.' I raised my eyebrows meaningfully, then went out to look at the abbey ruins, which were looking very spooky indeed in the moonlight. I could just, very faintly, see something glimmering. I was *sure* I could see something.

'Can you lend me your binoculars?' I asked Hannah.

She gave them to me and I adjusted them until I could see the abbey quite clearly. Yes! There were definitely spooky, flickering lights all in and out of the ruins, like tiny little candles going on and off.

Sasha and Sammy were back by now, and I showed them, too.

'Never mind about your aliens,' I said, 'there's some spooky lights in the abbey. That's absolute living proof of ghosts!'

'Oooh!' Sammy said.

'I'm not going near there!' Sasha said.

I lowered my voice. 'It's the monks

who once lived there. Holding their prayer-candles they're moving slowly through the church, reluctant to leave their dwelling-place on earth.'

Beezie came up looking like the Wild Woman of Wiltshire in her dressing-gown and hair, and I told her about them. It seemed as if she didn't believe me, but she shut up pretty swiftly when she'd peered through the binoculars. Miss Powling was in the next-door tent, hanging wild herbs in the proper position for positive forces or something, and Beezie called her in.

Miss Powling waved away the offer of binoculars. 'It's OK, I don't have to look,' she said. 'It's nothing supernatural—just fireflies.'

'What?' I said. 'It can't be. It's the candles of long-dead monks.'

'No, fireflies. Marvellous little creatures—we get them every year in that meadow. They flash to their mates from a special organ near their abdomens and the lights help male and female to locate each other.'

'Oh, really?' I muttered. I went inside and climbed into my sleeping-bag, full of gloom. *Fireflies.* You couldn't trust anything these days.

A full moon came out later, and to make good use of it I tried to scare the wits out of Sasha and Sammy, making a growling noise in the back of my throat which I gradually made louder and louder until it made me cough.

'Do you hear that?' I asked. 'It's full moon and that's a werewolf growling for his dinner.'

'What *is* his dinner?' Hannah asked. 'I hope it's not anything with feathers on.'

'No. He prefers humans,' I said throatily. I made another growling noise, wondering what werewolves did—apart from be all hairy. I didn't think they did anything specific—not like vampires or anything. Perhaps they just prowled about being hairy and howling at the moon. But that didn't seem very scary, somehow. Labradors did that.

'This is an especially horrible and wicked werewolf that rips people's heads off,' I went on, having decided to make it as scary as possible. 'And when it's completely ripped off their—' I turned my head as I spoke, then gave a sudden shriek of fright: Beezie was standing there looming above me, her Wild Woman's hair frizzed out all round her head.

'That's quite enough, Amy,' she said. 'I've had to speak to you about this several times already. I don't think the other girls need to know what werewolves do—not that there is such a thing anyway. It's not really what this camping trip is all about. It's about nature and history and getting a feeling for the land, not about trying to find ghosts or trying to scare the other girls to death.'

I blinked several times and gave my head a shake, as if I was trying to pull myself together. 'Oh, sorry, Miss Beasley,' I said. 'I must have been talking in my sleep.'

CHAPTER SIX

'I do believe . . .' I looked closer at the oak tree. 'I do believe there's something hidden in the trunk of this old tree.'

Sasha came up behind me. 'Is it a message from aliens?' she asked.

'No, it isn't,' I said shortly. I was fed up with aliens. All anyone had talked about for the last three days was the crop circles ('Why d'you think they do them? What are the aliens trying to tell us?') and you couldn't come out of your tent without a newspaper reporter calling over the hedge to ask, 'Which way to Hangman's Hill, please?' or zooming past you in an off-road vehicle and covering you with dust. I hadn't even been able to get up to the alien landing-spot because Mrs Emmet said we were to keep away from there, and although I'd tried and tried to wake up in the middle of the night and go out and have an adventure at the abbey, I still hadn't managed to do it.

‘What is it, then?’ Sasha asked now. I waited, wanting to get Sammy’s attention as well. I never believe in doing things by halves.

‘Well, I do believe it’s an OLD TREASURE MAP,’ I said loudly.

Sammy, who’d been sticking something boring into her project-book, looked up.

‘What is?’

‘Yes. An old treasure map,’ I repeated. I pulled it out. It was drawn on ancient parchment (or as ancient as I’d been able to make it) and showed the next field to us, which was a ploughed-up one, with an ‘X marks the spot’ and various symbols and signs. I’d seen treasure maps in my books and I knew what they were supposed to look like. I’d brought everything with me from home to make it, and had spent ages that morning sitting in the Portaloo working on it. I’d made the edges curled and wrinkled, and added various things like *To ye river* and *Ye olde bushe* and a nice compass sign in purple and blue showing where north was. All down the side I’d written instructions for finding it: *Starting at the gate, take four paces to the right, six left, turn round, take away the number you first thought of, take five steps due north,* etc. It didn't actually make much sense, but that hardly mattered when it wasn't real anyway.

'Oh, wow!' Sasha said, looking over my shoulder. 'Is it real?'

'Course!' I assured her, busily crossing my fingers.

'Let's start digging, then,' Sammy said.

'All in good time.' I brandished the map. 'I found it so I'm the one in charge of the expedition.'

'What expedition? Are you going far?' Hannah asked, coming out of our tent.

'Not really. Just in the next field,' I said.

'Only, I heard you say "expedition" so I thought you might be going across the desert or into the jungle or somewhere.'

'We've got an ancient treasure map!' Sasha said.

'X marks the spot!' said Sammy.

'Oh. And who found it?' Hannah asked. 'Was it you, Amy, by any chance?'

'It might have been,' I said. 'Anyway, do you want to hunt for treasure with us or not?'

'I don't mind,' Hannah said. 'It would be something to do.' Even she'd had her fill of the wonders of nature. As for me, I still hadn't got *anything* in my project-book. I was even thinking of pretending to like birds so I could pinch some stuff off Hannah.

'Right then,' I said, and was just about to start them all pacing across to work out 'X marks the spot' when Miss Powling came over to us.

'We're all going dipping!' she said.

We looked at her without enthusiasm.

'Everyone's to bring a jamjar and we're going to dip them in the river and see what we can find.'

'But Amy's just found a—'

I exploded in an avalanche of coughing, shaking my head warningly at Sasha. I didn't want any of the teachers to get a glimpse of the treasure map. They'd see through it in seconds.

Miss Powling clapped her hands to bring us all to attention. 'Come along!' she said. 'Through the gateway and down the path towards the river.'

We did as we were told and I was quite glad of the breathing space, actually, because I hadn't yet decided what the treasure was going to be. I'd brought some old dressing-up beads with me that I'd had when I was little, but I wasn't convinced they looked like treasure. Not the sort of treasure you see in pictures when they lift up the lid of an ancient wooden chest and it's there, all sparkling and shimmering, gold coins overflowing. This was more red and white plastic beads and wide, green shiny bracelets. Thoughtfully, I put the map back in the tree and followed Hannah and the others through the gate.

We walked down the edge of the next field and then across another. Since we all knew that the demon farmer was now the ex-demon farmer, and Julia had been revealed as his niece, everyone was a bit more laid back about walking across fields.

The third field had some big granite stones in it, and Miss Powling paused halfway across, flinging her arms wide as if introducing something.

'These are standing stones,' she said in a serious, hushed voice.

I frowned. 'But some of them are lying down sideways.'

'Nevertheless, Amy, they are called standing stones,' she said.

'I don't see why when they're—'

'That's enough,' she said. She went over and placed her hand on them. 'Feel! Feel three thousand years' worth of history beneath your fingertips.'

I felt. I couldn't.

'What is it supposed to feel like?' I asked.

She turned her back on me and spoke to the others. 'Look at the lichen, the moss, the tiny little growing things. Look at Mother Nature at her most subtle!'

Beezie's hair stepped forward with her underneath it. 'These stones are called The Seven Judges. They're supposed to be seven wise men who were turned into stone.'

I perked up a bit. *This* was more like it.

'There's a stone up at the abbey that's a monk who was turned into stone,' I volunteered.

'Really?' Beezie said. 'I hadn't heard about that.'

'It's only recently been discovered,' I said. Everyone was looking at me expecting more, so I went on hurriedly, 'He was turned into stone because . . . because he made the abbot's tea wrong.'

Behind me I heard Sammy and Sasha giggle.

'Oh, really, Amy,' Beezie said.

Hannah whispered, 'That's not a very good reason.'

'It was all I could think of at the time,' I whispered back.

'To go back to these stones that we actually know about,' Beezie went on. 'These seven men were turned to stone because they caused a witch to be put to death.'

'Wow!' I said, nudging Hannah and

anyone else within nudging distance.

'And legend has it that once a year, on the anniversary of the death of the witch, the judges move.'

'Fantastic!' I said. Someone had obviously been reading the same books as I had.

'Although no one has ever seen them,' she continued.

'It doesn't mean they don't!' I said. 'I bet they do. I bet when no one's looking they walk around the place all the time.'

'And now let's move on and down to the river,' Miss Powling said, opening the next gate. 'Let us take in the energy of the running water!'

I looked back, reluctant to leave The Seven Judges. 'I think I can see one moving,' I said. 'I'm sure one just wriggled its head a bit.'

But no one took any notice of me and we went on down to the river, while I gave some serious thought to what bits of treasure we were going to find.

CHAPTER SEVEN

The dipping was as boring as I thought it was going to be, although I did spot a floating log and got everyone going by saying it was a Loch Ness monster, but that only lasted about half a minute. Miss Powling found water boatmen and dragonflies and sticklebacks and a frog and a diving beetle, but I didn't find anything.

When we got back to camp everyone was supposed to go back to their tents and write up about the river dipping and what they'd discovered. I hadn't discovered anything so I left them all to it and went outside, taking with me a funny old sparkly necklace that had once belonged to my Auntie Jean. I decided to take the box it came in, too. This, I thought, would stop the sparkles getting covered in mud, and also having a box to open would add to the excitement. Hiding it up my sleeve, I went through the gate into the next field and hid it in a hawthorn bush.

(The communing-with-nature business must have done something for me, because I knew it was a hawthorn bush.)

I then went back to the others in our tent. 'I've just been looking at the old treasure map again,' I said. 'I think we might have some serious digging to do.'

* * *

Half an hour later we were making good progress. The treasure map had been studied and, because it was so vague, we were digging holes with sticks and our hands all over the place and getting covered in mud. I say all—that is, Hannah, Sasha, Sammy and me as well—because I'd got so keen on the idea of buried treasure that I'd almost forgotten that I'd made up the map in the first place. We kept moving to new areas and digging new holes, and soon we'd found some bits of flint, a few old bones—Hannah said they were sheep bones—a rusty disc thing and some pieces of pottery. When Sasha dug up a lump of iron and the others gathered round to try and guess what it was, I stealthily made my way to the hawthorn bush.

'I wonder if it's over this way,' I muttered, pretending to look into a ditch but actually getting hold of the necklace box. I walked a few steps further on, saw a rabbit hole and shoved it in, then went back to the others.

I pretended to study the map again. 'I've just got an idea the treasure's over this way,' I said. 'Somewhere around'—I waved my arm around and then pointed in the direction I wanted them to go—'*there*!'

Dutifully they made their way to this new spot. We put the map on the ground and all the finds on top of it. Much as I wanted to, I thought it would be best not to actually discover the real treasure myself, so I sort of pointed at it with my right foot and pretended to look all round me. 'It's somewhere round here, I think,' I said. 'I've just got this feeling about it.' I put my hand to my head. 'I feel it's something to do with the abbey . . . the monks were in danger and had to bury their treasure quickly . . . I think it's about here.'

Hannah had spotted something birdy in the hedge by this time so was distracted, and it took ages for either of the other two, scrabbling around with their sticks, to notice anything—in the end I practically had to push their noses in it. At last Sasha gave a squeal.

'I've got it!' she said. 'Here it is! Here's the buried treasure!'

She pulled it out of the rabbit hole and brushed the dirt off.

'Oh! Fancy *you* finding it! Lucky!' I said. 'Oh, quickly, let's look inside!'

We all gathered around, even Hannah.

'Imagine . . . hundreds of years ago the monks were attacked and had to hide their treasure,' I said. 'And then I found their actual map.'

The lid of the box was opened and everyone gasped. Me especially loudly. 'Gold and diamonds!' I cried.

There was a moment's silence.

'But . . . but why would a monk have a diamond necklace?' Hannah asked then.

'I don't know,' I said. 'Perhaps they had fancy dress parties or something.'

'And why does it say inside the box: *Masons, Modern Jewellers*?'

'I've no idea!' I said irritably. 'You can't expect me to know everything about monks and where they do their shopping.'

'Girls! Coo-ee!'

We looked up to see Beezie at the gate. I think she must have just washed her hair because it looked huger than ever, as if it was taking her over.

'You're not supposed to be in there, girls! You know that field is out of bounds.'

'But there's no crop in it,' I said.

'Miss! We've found treasure!' Sasha cried.

'Sort of,' Hannah added.

Beezie opened the gate and my heart sank. As far as I was concerned it hadn't been a very good week, what with the Wildcat of Wiltshire being discovered to be cardboard, the candles of the long-dead monks turning out to be fireflies and the crop circles turning out to have been made by me. And now Beezie was bound to ruin my ancient-treasure-map event.

She swooped down on us. 'Where did you get *that*?' she cried.

'It was hidden in the earth,' Sasha said.

'And we found the map in a tree,' Sammy said. 'At least, Amy did. And we followed the instructions and dug and we found—'

'I think it's Roman!' Beezie said excitedly.

I goggled at her. No, it's *Auntie's*, I felt like saying.

But she wasn't looking at the necklace. She was holding the rusty old disc thing.

'A Roman coin. A *denarius*.' She held it up between finger and thumb. 'Silver, I think, and I can see some clear markings and an emperor's head. I know a little bit about coins and I think this is quite rare, so we'd better get it to a museum. It's definitely treasure-trove.'

'Oh, wow! Treasure-trove,' I said. I thought quickly. 'I bet this is what the map was supposed to lead to—not the necklace at all.'

'How did that necklace come to be here, then?' Sammy asked.

'It was just a red herring,' I said.

'What's that mean?' Sasha said. 'Someone must have put it there.' She looked at me very hard. *'Someone . . .'*

'Ssshh. Miss Beasley's speaking!' I said to her severely.

'Yes, this is really most interesting,' Beezie said, luckily not even glancing at the map or the necklace.

'Is that coin worth a lot of money?' Hannah asked.

'It may well be,' Beezie said. 'But as treasure-trove it becomes the property of the crown and you have to give it up.'

'Does that mean we don't get anything for it?' I asked.

'Well, if it's given up you get the amount of money which the treasure would fetch if it was sold. Unfortunately, before you start planning what you'll buy, you should know that this coin is deemed to belong to the person who owns the land,' Beezie said.

We all groaned. 'That's not fair!'

'Isn't it finders keepers?' Hannah asked.

Beezie shook her head. 'Afraid not,' she said. 'That is, unless the landowner—that'll be Miss Dean—passes her rights to you. And I can't see any reason why she should, can you?'

As I thought about this, there was a rustle from the other side of the hedge and we looked towards it. After a moment Julia appeared with two pairs of binoculars around her neck.

'Oh, hello,' she said. 'Excuse me creeping around, but there's possibly a redpoll around here.'

A squeal of delight came from Hannah.

'Miss Dean,' Beezie called. 'I'm pleased you've turned up. I've got some rather good news for you—I believe my girls have found a Roman coin in your field.'

'Really?' Julia said. She was looking up a tree, though, not at us.

'I've told them that you, of course, as the landowner, actually have ownership of it.'

Julia looked over and seemed to see me for the first time. 'Oh, hello, Amy,' she said, and I said 'Hello' back.

Beezie held the coin out to Julia and she came over and took it. 'Well, how interesting,' she said, holding it this way and that. 'I've never seen one of these before. Not to actually hold, I mean.'

'It's a *denarius,* I think,' Beezie said. 'Rather a good specimen and so worth a fair bit of money.'

'Is it really?' Julia said. 'Lucky old me.'

I'd been thinking with superhuman speed, and now I cleared my throat and coughed delicately. 'Have any more crop circles appeared lately?' I asked, and then I winked at Julia, just the way she'd winked at me the day the reporters had appeared.

She hesitated. She knew exactly what I was getting at. 'No,' she said slowly. 'No more crop circles at the moment.'

'Funny, that,' I said, and I shook my head in a mystified sort of way. 'Funny how they appeared just out of nowhere.

And we were in that field only the day before, too, and didn't notice a thing!'

Beezie glanced at me, hair on one side, as if she was trying to work out what I was getting at. I just carried on looking at Julia, wearing my inscrutable expression, and after a moment she looked at Beezie and said, 'I think, actually, that your school ought to keep the coin. Perhaps you'd like to sell it and buy some books for the library.'

'Hurray!' I said under my breath.

'Well, how very generous of you!' said Beezie.

Julia looked at me as if weighing me up. 'And please let Amy choose them,' she added.

'That's most kind of you, Miss Dean,' Beezie said. 'Thank you very much.'

I beamed at Julia, then I beamed at Beezie and the others. 'Treasure-trove!' I said. 'Lots of books for the school library. And all thanks to me. OK, I'm going to get lots of ghost books and vampire books and werewolf books and books about witches.' I looked at Julia. 'And maybe one on crop circles as well, and how they come to be formed.'

Julia laughed. So did I. I decided that it had been a pretty good week after all and I knew exactly what I was going to do. When I got back to the tent I was going to rename my nature diary and call it SPOOK SUMMER.